TELEPHONE

Ariana   Reines

W

TELEPHONE was commissioned by The Foundry Theatre and
produced at the Cherry Lane Theatre in New York, February 6-28,
2009. The Telephone Book by Avital Ronell is the play's inspiration.

TELEPHONE was first published in PLAY: A JOURNAL OF PLAYS,
edited by Sylvan Oswald and Jordan Harrison, in 2010.

The Introduction by Chris Kraus was first published in
Spike Quarterly, Berlin, in 2009.

First Printing
Published by Wonder
www.shitwonder.com

Cover by Mary Austin Speaker
Layout by Joel Gregory
978-0-9895985-8-3

Printed in the United States

In memory of Mark Anthony Wilson

TELEPHONE

INTRODUCTION

"When you hang up, [the telephone] does not disappear but goes into remission,"

- Avital Ronell

~~~~~~~~~~~~~~~~~~~

Published in pre-internet 1989, *The Telephone Book — Technology, Schizophrenia, Electric Speech* is beyond brilliant; prescient. A Derridean meditation, Ronell's book is both a history of the telephone's invention and a historiography of inferences that have been drawn from it. Through its disembodied voice, Ronell writes, "the telephone ... globalizes and unifies, suturing a country like a wound ... A state casts a net of connectedness around itself from which the deadly flower of unity can grow under the sun of constant surveillance." At the same time, "the telephone has been the schizophrenic's darling ... spanning indivisible distances ... it donated structures of disconnection and long-range close distance."

Dense, difficult, moving wildly back and forth across the threshold of the comprehensible, *The Telephone Book* hardly seems adaptable as a play, much less as an Off-Broadway production staged in the West Village at the tradition-steeped Cherry Lane Theatre. Granted, Ronell is a performative philosopher, but Ariana Reines' play, boldly commissioned by The Foundry Theatre, distills the interruptive cacophony of Ronell's argument into something that's hilarious and dirge-like. *Telephone* is a deadpan eulogy for the pre-emptive affects of technology.

Reines, a former student of Ronell's, has reinvented poetry for the contemporary art world with her recent books *The Cow* (2006) and *Coeur de Lion* (2007). Her books are models of punk erudition — manifestos of the paradoxical girl-state where disappearance beckons through to presence, and you are completely alert to a point where you can no longer stand it. Deceptively simple, her script discerns the schizophrenic state that technology brings into being.

In Act I (1876), Alexander Graham Bell and Thomas Watson, played by Gibson Frazier and Matthew Dellapina as Beckett-like clowns in frock coats, are exuberant in their invention of the telephone. But soon they discover how slippery words become when transmitted "electro-magnetically". The telephone's first utterance — "Watson come here I want you" — is already suspect. Neither can remember if the word Bell used was "need" or "want" and does the difference matter? "I want", says Bell, "to know how faithfully it was transmitted". Transmission usurps meaning. But what did Bell's voice *sound* like? All Watson can recall is "a small man. calling forth from deep. in a. in a. barrel. of brine ... like. the darkness. being divided. from the light." The dawning of the 20th century ... technological Genesis.

Act 2 is an encounter with Miss St., a former dressmaker who was admitted to a mental institution in 1887, torn apart by voices that she heard over the invisible telephones she perceived to be installed within her body. A patient of Carl Jung's, she complained of "hieroglyphic suffering". Spot-lit on a table, wearing an elaborate bustle and bent over a walking stick, the sight of Birgit Huppuch's Miss St. first recalls one of Charcot's asylum photographs. In an astonishing 35 minute solo, Huppuch courses through the range of madness, from surfeit to exhaustion to depleted loneliness.

Which is where Reines' contemporary characters begin Act 3. Talking on their cell phones, texting into chat rooms, their communication as non-sequitous as life:

> *I don't want to explain myself./Okay./I just ... I just want to talk to somebody who already understands me. I want to talk to somebody who feels me./Do you have an idea of who this person might be?/Well? You maybe? (silence) Uhm.*

The technologic state of autism endlessly fed back, cool and heart-rending.

- CHRIS KRAUS

{{{{}}}}
{{{{}}}}
{should}}
{{{{we}}
{{begin}}
{{{let}}}
{{{{us}}
{{agree}}
{{{{}}}}
{{{{}}}}

{note}

~~~~~~~~~~~~~~~~~~~~~

If there is light it is divided from the darkness.
If there is sound it is invested with silence.

The silence is filled with qualities.

The room fills slowly with qualities. The room fills up with silence.

Slowly the room becomes this.

If there is light it is divided from the darkness.

If a voice speaks it is divided from the silence.

It should feel darker and more silent than it is.

Like walking into a room that is not your room, that is not your home, or a room that is your new home, and not knowing where the lightswitch is, or whether there is one, and what if somebody is there.

What if there is somebody in there, waiting for you in the dark.

The audience should have a feeling of care and apprehension and arousal inside their bodies.

The actors exude this care and apprehension and arousal.

We could think of this beginning like the beginning of Das Rheingold, a beginning of the world. But not gold: black. Not water nymphs: currents.

Primoridal electricity.

Sensitive electricity.

Delicacy.

Thickness.

Thick dark.
Let us go

from house lights

to gradual darkness

to absolute darkness.

From inaudible silence

to gradually

audible silence:

~~~~~~~~~~~~~~~~~~

Darkness.

Time passes.

Silence; darkness.

Electrical current.

A muffled sound.

A muffled sound.

A cluster of muffled sounds.

Low frequency.

Keypads; buttons. Little puttings. Sounds of small physical things.

Soft sound of something soft dropped onto a carpet. A few times, layered together, a little denser.

Flower petals torn.

Fabric torn.

Little sounds; dull.

Little springs, little twangs, edges of sounds.

Things that almost sound like something.

Some vibrations. They oscillate, vibrate more.

Cellphones on vibrate.

A click.

A lick.

Some clicks.

Digital clicks. Physical ones.

*Buttons and things, snaps and closures. Twangs.
Something hollow, something opaque.*

Getting a little louder.

Consolidating somewhat.

*Increasing implications; thicker sounds; or a thicker
layering of thin, small, still small sounds.*

A tone.

Low tone.

Oh, low tone opens,

Broadens.

A sound that could be an O sounding but only almost.

*All the while the gradual crescendo is happening, is a
consolidation, gathering in.*

Upon the tone build others, out of deaf sounds, dull bells.
A shiver, a shimmer, a cluster of shaking bells.

A mess of them. More.

Bells are gone.

Bells are not gone.

Dense frequency now.

Some bells and the undersides of what they sound like,
their overtones, This is allowed to be very beautiful.

Bells begin to seem to be in a rhythm. This lasts for only a
few seconds. Then they are messy again.

Into this mess maybe a smattering of voices. Everyday
intonations.

Voices we will have recorded.

A trough or column of voices, voice parts, hacked up,
assonance, intonation, familiar fragments of how people
sound, starting to feel strange, more distant, more distant
and more ominous.

Noise.

Maybe a sound of singing, or several singing sounds in a
column, a chord. A discordant chord that is not discordant
at the end.

Maybe a triumphant note for a while, but then it climbs
higher and higher, more chaotic,

A scream. A din. Or not

01   Watson and Bell

~~~~~~~~~~~~~~~~~~~~~~

vaudeville

B   WATSON COME HERE I WANT YOU

Light. WATSON and BELL frozen.

Table. Telephone equipment. Tuning fork. Wall.
Painting of owl on it. Two chairs.

silence
silence
silence

B   Wait wait wait wait wait wait

silence
silence
silence

W   What. You want me to go?

silence

B   No no—ah. *silence* Stay. But – wait wait—

B   What is it.

B   It worked!

W   Yes?

B   Yes yes!

W   Yes yes yes! Oh Bell! Do you remember June 2,

1875, when we proved that different tones vary the strength of an electric current in a wire, just as they vary the movement of the air?

B   Yes indeed! My harmonic telegraph! Yes!

W   My twanging spring! Your harmonic telegraph! Yes! And now?

B   Electric speech! The method of, and apparatus for, transmitting vocal or other sounds telegraphically! By reproducing—electrically— the vibrations in the air as caused by human speech! The transportation of sound via electrical undulations, the form of which match the vibrations upon the air, the vibrations caused by vocal—or other—sound!!!

W   Yes yes!!!!

B   Once a voice spoke to Moses through a burning bush!

W   And now! any home or office can have a burning bush of its own! Any voice can be freed from the encumbrance of its body! Free to travel miles and miles, over land and sea!

B   Yes yes! But—But Wait! Watson. what did you hear!

W   Oh!

B   What did you hear! Over the electromagnetic receiver! What did it sound like! On the electromagnetic receiver!

W   Well. *silence* Complicated. Complex.

B   Watson. Just say what I said. Just tell me what you heard.

W   I heard *silence* a lot of things. A great many things.

B   Such as

W   I don't know where to start.

B   What about my voice

W   Yes.

B   Yes what?

W   Yes I heard your voice.

B   You're sure you heard it.

W   Yes Alec.

B   What did it sound like?

W   Like. Well. It sounded. Like.

          silence
          silence
          silence

B   Like?

W   A. *silence* A small man. Calling forth from deep.
          In a. In a. Barrel. Of brine. Like. A thrush. In a
          metal can on, ah, upon the foaming sea. *silence*
          Uh. Like. The darkness. Being divided. From the
          light.

B	Like what?
W	Like the darkness being divided from the light.
B	Really?
W	And. Like. Like the insides of the throats of, of, of hornets. If hornets had throats. And reverberating. As though inside a single metal teat. Metal teat. You know, like a rubber teat, but metal. Like a bell.
B	Please Watson.
W	Yes Bell.
B	Did you even hear what I said.
W	I'm here aren't I
B	Watson. Tell me what I said.
W	Watson. You said Watson. Come here I want you. Ah. Wait. Actually what you said was. Um. Watson come here I need you. Uh—
B	Need or want.
W	Either one.
B	Didn't you hear me say it?
W	Yes.
B	So which was it? Want or need.
W	What would you say the difference is. Is there a difference?

B   Did you or did you not hear me say it.

W   I heard you.

B   And?

W   Don't YOU remember what you said?

B   Naturally. But I want to know how faithfully it was transmitted.

W   *silence* I am sure. It was. *silence* Either want or need—Want. It was want. You said Watson come here I want you.

B   I want to see you?

W   No just. I want you. You don't remember do you.

B   I—I um. Oh. Well. Of course I remember. Or,
          almost, I mean, only, or rather—
          I wanted you to come here.

W   I know.

B   Naturally.

W   Well then.

B   Here you are.

W   Yes.

B   Hello.

W   Hello how are you.

B   Fine thank you how are you.

W   Splendid, thank you, so kind of you to ask. And
          how is the sheepbreeding getting on. Still splicing
          nipples? Ho ho! How is the family?

          silence
          silence
          silence

B   Family. My brothers? They're dead. Two of my
          boys were? Are. Consumption.

W   Oh my

B   Well.

W   Tuberculosis.

B   Yah. *silence silence silence* I fashioned something to help them but.

W   What did you make.

B   Well. A kind of. Buttress. A breathing machine. You know a. Supplement. I fashioned a kind of metal vacuum jacket. Like a kind of lung.

W   Did it work

B   It worked. But it. It did not save my boys.

W   I wonder whether. Whether machines ever feel lonely for the people they were fashioned to assist.

B   I do not think that inanimate objects feel, Watson.

W   And yet there is feeling in them.

B   If there is feeling in them, we put it there.

W   Feeling can pass through a thing.

B   Mm. Yes.

W   What I am saying is I want more life.

B   Go on.

W   I feel more life than I have.

B   Say again?

W   I feel more life. Than I. Possess.

B   You feel more life than you possess?

silence
silence
silence

W   Uh. *silence* Leave it. Nevermind.

B   What do you mean. Possess.

W   I-ah. it is too private. i don't know how to say it.

B   Watson?

W   Yes Bell.

B   It seems we might not have undertaken this properly.

W   I think we're managing reasonably well.

B   You do?

W   I came, did I not?

B   Yes you did.

W   So it was intelligible. You wanted me to come, did you not?

B   Yes I did. *silence silence silence*

          So. We have made history.

W	It gives me a sensation of distance to have done so.
B	There was an emergency. I thought.
W	Yes. Well, naturally. That's what it's for.
B	Hm?
W	Telephone. It's for emergencies.
B	Yes well I was in a bit of a pickle.
W	You were visibly excited, yes.
B	Rather. Or – rather. It was. A fever.
W	Do you feel ill?
B	No you know just the ah. Inventing fever. Electric speech! It was mad!
W	Alexander Graham Bell! The man who contracted space!
B	Ahem.
W	*silence, as though awaiting applause*
B	Well ah. I couldn't have contracted space if um. If you hadn't been on the ah. Other end of the. Space.

W	*silence*
B	I could not have – I mean, rather, We could not have. Done it. Without you.
W	Thank you.
B	No thank YOU.
W	No YOU. Thank YOU! ALEC!
B	Yes yes. WE DID IT!
W	WE'VE DONE IT!
W+B	WAR DANCE!

they do a loud 'war dance'
BELL breaks off, stares at his chest.

B	I seem to have spilled this all over myself.
W	What.
B	Battery acid. Sloshed out of the transmitter.
W	When?
B	When I called you. I think.
W	Doesn't it hurt?
B	I don't know. I suppose so.
W	Bell. Are you alright.
B	I think so.
W	That acid. Ought I to help you off with your clothes. *silence*
	Alec?
B	Hmm. I suppose. Uh. Not unless we're going for a swim. Haha. *silence* O Canada.
W	Hm?
B	Watson
W	Yes
B	Is this Canada.

silence

W   *slowly* I don't know

silence

B   I don't. Feel quite at home.

W   You don't?

B   *calling out* Mabel? *silence silence silence* Darling? *silence silence silence* Not that she can hear me. Unless she's looking at me.

B   Watson. Where are we.

W   *silence* I think—*silence*—that's immaterial.

B   Watson.

W   I think. *silence* We are in the universe.

B   Genius, Watson.

W   Well? Whenever I think of Canada, a feeling of unreality overtakes me. I imagine a reality that resembles mine, but which is not mine. I have always felt this way about Canada.

B   That's quite common. It's because you are American. Canada may be high, but it is real.

W   You know what, Bell? I do feel rather elevated. Does the air smell like Canada to you?

B   *breathes* I am not sure. *breathes* Canada's quite vast, of course. All kinds of airs. *breathes* I don't think this *breathes* is Ontario air.

W   It's air though.

B   I think so.

W   So we must be somewhere.

B   Mmff. Did you conjure me?

W   I rather think it was you who conjured me.

B   I invent. I do not conjure.

W Was there an emergency? Is there one?

B The emergency is. Well. The emergency is. Thank you for coming.

W   Thank YOU for calling, rather.

B   My pleasure. Thank YOU.

W   Well, ah. Wherever I am I am still I. Right? That is my joy and my misery. I am still I. That's like waiting. To become. Something other. Or. Like. Waiting by the phone. *silence* On your behalf. It's like living. Waiting to sing "Do Not Trust Him Gentle Lady".

B   I beg your pardon?

W   I'm talking about being somewhere. Waiting. By the phone.

B   Please, Watson. Where are we.

W   Bell. What did you call me for.

B   I was in a state of excitement and distress.

W   Over what.

B   Well as you saw I spilled the battery acid.

W   But what about before you called. What about right before.

B   I don't know. I just. I just did what I do. I do something. About something. We do. *silence* Watson. *silence*

W   Alright, alright, excellent. And this. This does something about something.

B   It has many uses.

W   What about friendship?

B   Certainly, if one friend is far away from another.

W   Is a friend a friend if that friend is a distant friend?

B   Now Watson. It's a small world, after all.

W   Bell. What would you say we are doing right now.

B   We are talking to one another in a friendly way.

W   Right. *silence*

B   And our device is an extension of this. But I don't see how this solves—

W   —Just hang on, Bell. You say our device is an extension. Of talking in a friendly way.

B   An amplification. Of fellow feeling. Our device. The telephone, it seems to me Watson, should make bigotry impossible. It shall. And render war unlikely, if not impossible. *silence* People will understand one another.

W   Right Bell, right! We're really getting somewhere now!

B   Where. Where are we getting.

W   Wait—wait, just wait Bell. Bell Pretend I am Socrates. Alright?

B   *sighs*

W   Alright. Suppose you are a lonely man. Who does not own a telephone.

B   What are you saying.

W   Suppose you are a lonely man who does not own a telephone.

B   Alright.

W   Then you are a lonely man.

B   Tautology.

W Nevertheless. Suppose you are a lonely man. Who owns a telephone.

B Yes?

W And nobody ever calls.

B Oh.

W Or if somebody ever calls. Something interferes. Bell. Perhaps one person cannot hear or understand the other or both people cannot understand each other, or the one says things in such a way that the other cannot understand either because of himself, something in himself, in his—his Essential Being!—or because of the way the one has said what he has said, and perhaps some of what one says makes sense and perhaps it makes so much sense that the other one cannot bear it, or both begin to panic and behave as though they hate one another but perhaps really it is the frustration of failing to reach some concord, something both can partake of, each thing the one proposes the other says But no it is not like that it is like this, perhaps some people argue and this expresses love and some people agree and this expresses morbid resignation, all those nights I waited for you making ready my singing repertory, and wouldn't you say Alec that there could be more required to cause one person to agree—to agree in a—in a—a spiritual way—with another, more required for this than having set up a proper machine and—and. And.

B	And what.
W	And pronouncing all the words correctly.
B	Of course. Tone. Timbre.
W	I'm talking about COMMUNICATION. What we made.
B	We did not make communication. We made 'COMMUNICATION**S**'.
W	We did not make COMMUNICATION**S**. Sam Morse made that. *pulls a voice* WHAT HATH GOD WROUGHT.
B	Morse did not make COMMUNICATION**S**. Gutenburg did.
W	Hieroglyphics.
B	Cuneiform.
W	Shakespeare.
B	Mother Goose.
W	Paul Revere.
B	*strikes tuning fork*
B	I don't know. Watson. Are we old or young?

W   *silence* I think we're somewhere in the middle.

B   What if we're dead. *silence silence silence*
Though I suppose in that case we should be with
the others. Should we not?

W   If you say so. It doesn't make much difference
to me really. You know. At least I have a mouth. I
could put a song in it. Hey Bell? The air's in my
mouth. My tongue is.

B   Mmmm. Mine too. Perhaps we are somewhat
more electric now than before. Sort of
electronically preserved, or—

W   Yes, electric is possible. Why not, somewhat?

B   Air is inconstant, but it is where we are.

W   Right. *silence silence* But silence we are not
smoke. We are not light. Are we? We are not,
not music or. Or wind! But then again—now and
again—I feel—you know? On occasion I must
admit that I DO feel myself to be a. A beam of
light. –On occasion. Or like a. A! Wind! As though
I am translated! Into something! You know?
Something. Overtakes me. On my Sundays in the
woods. It's like nature. But—extra. A second.
Nature. I mean. I slip into a kind of.

B   I know.

W   Just wait. I'm saying. A kind of dreamy bliss.
The contents of which I feel powerless to put
into words. If I had a friend who was disposed
to understanding my way of expressing things,

perhaps in time I could learn express some of them by extra-verbal means. I tried to learn the piano but I could not master it. I bought myself a horse but it did not like me. I can't—I can't— TRANSMIT myself.

B   Well. You are now.

W   No, I'm not. I'm failing.

B   You are expressing your failure. In English.

W   I'm trying.

B   Yes.

W   But. If nobody knows what I'm saying. Then I might as well be mute.

B   I'm right in front of you. I can hear you. I'm not deaf.

W   Not hear. Understand.

B   I understand.

W   You understand the words. There's—there's more than that.

B   I taught elocution for years. I know.

W   No I mean—something obscure. Something vast! Oceanic!

B   What?

W   *wretched silence silence silence*

B   You want this thing to be inexpressible. It need not be. Reach out and touch someone. It's not impossible.

W   But. Isn't it? Sometimes? Isn't it always a question. *Silence.* Hello? *Silence.* Yes?

B   The human, even the deaf human, is no longer quite so alone.

W   Not all the time.

B   *Getting a little grandiose* And those in distress... Whatever.

W   I see the terrifying spaces of the universe
hemming me in.

Watson and Bell look at each other.

W   Pascal. rueful laugh. *silence silence silence* I
think I could. With patience. Discern a thread of
something in the air that might indicate how we
are where we are, and perhaps why, and remind
you why you said you wanted me, perhaps it's a
manner of speaking, elegant nostalgia, to repeat
what you once said to me you in one room and
I in another. I would like time. I take my time. I
could learn and recognize and note the qualities
of this--atmosphere. Then we could build an
instrument that could scan the air, see what there
is to hear. I feel sure there is more here. –

B   More what.

W   More than what we know. More everything. More
being. More happening.

B   And you expect to ascertain what this "more" is
merely by listening.

W   Well? Not merely. I mean. Yes, Alec.

B   Suppose you did hear something. How could you
know that it wasn't just a, a touch of tinnitus, you
know? Suppose you did hear something. How could
you possibly deduce with any coherence that it
absolutely was NOT just a reverberation in yourself.
A fact of of, of your own ear. Hearing itself.

W   If I were to hear something, then I'd bring it to your attention. You would hear it too.

B   Alright, fine. Let's give it a whirl then. If you hear
something noteworthy, give me a holler.

silence
silence
silence

W	*miserable* You used to be different
B	Speech is silver, silence is golden.
W	Once the morning-glories talked to me in their language and it was intelligible to me.
B	You know something Watson? It's labor to maintain one's integrity the whole length of a life. You know. Just to be a single person. It's. Exhausting. How do people do it. How do they. Remain themselves. I mean. I had to get ill all the time, didn't I. And take the airs. Convalesce. Just to remain the same person. To become a person and to remain one. To be an uncontaminated person. I mean, one minute you're settling down into yourself. And the next you are consumed by. By. Some phenomenon. Gesturing at the telephone. I don't even like the thing. Clumsy.
	silence
W	*trying* Bell. Can you see me glowing?
B	Watson.
W	My halo. Oh well. *maybe make this big, a big gesture or moment in W's body— spirituality*
B	I'm trying.
W	In any case you never could see it even when it was here, assuming it's not here now. Is it here?
B	I can't see it.

W   Nevertheless it might be here.

B   sigh It might well be. Invisible but here. I have kept an open mind on the subject, you know. I always endeavor to believe you. And even when I cannot quite believe. I try to understand.

Bell starts humming

W   I'm so—*curses himself with obscenities, under breath*—Sorry—

W   Bell.

B   Uh uh.

W   How do you feel Bell.

B   Oh. Uh. Uh. I feel. 1 2 3 4 5 6 7. 1 2 3 4 5 6
7. 1 2 3 4 5 6 7. Uh. 8 9 10 11 12. Oh one oh
one one one one one oh one. Oh oh. One OH one oh
one oh one. ONE oh oh ONE oh ONE one ONE oh.
What is love baby don't hurt me. Don't hurt me.
No more. Woh ooh woh ooh wohoowohoh. Etc

silence
silence
silence

W   Bell you could make it a little easier on me. You
could help me a little.

B   I am not preventing you.

W   From what.

B   From anything. You are the one who wants to be
Socrates.

W   Bell, maybe we should call someone.

B   Hmm. There's an idea. *silence* You know. When
I was a boy? My brother Melly and I made a
promise to each other. That should one of us die,
the other would try to contact him.

W   How?

B   I'm not sure that in our boyishness we really
knew.

W	So what happened, Bell?
B	Well? Melly died.
W	And?
B	And? I don't know.
W	You don't know?
B	I don't know.

W	Did you try to reach him?
B	*silence silence silence*
W	We could explore this! We could call him!
B	My brother?
W	Why not?
B	Don't insult me Watson.
W	I'm not! I'm not!
B	That was – boyish fancy.
W	Perhaps.
B	What would we say. What do we have to say.
W	*sounds artificial* Hello how are you.
B	Is this an emergency? Do we need help?
W	Maybe! Maybe we need help!
B	Watson, you don't find this the least bit grotesque?
W	Well? Not necessarily.
B	Mmmh.
W	We could call someone! Anyone. We could disguise our voices. You would have to. You're famous. You might intimidate people. I wonder if

| | we could talk to an operator. |
| **B** | What would she say. |

| **W** | We could say something dirty to her. Or have her connect us to someone and, just pretend to be. Conducting a political survey. |

| **B** | Do you suppose these are even connected. |

| **W** | Other than— FUCK. To one another. |

silence

| **B** | Perhaps we're being punished. |

| **W** | For what. |

| **B** | For... interfering with God's work. If the lord had meant to house speech in machines, he would not have given us tongues. Or whatever. Nevermind. I don't know. |

| **W** | Bell. Why don't we pick up where we left off |

| **B** | What. |

| **W** | Why don't we pick up where we left off, and keep going? |

| **B** | Keep going? |

| **W** | Yes. |

silence

W Bell? Bell. I used to hear things.

B What?

W I have heard things. at night in your loft. I used to hear these delicate things. At night Bell. I mean. Right here. I would sit up and listen to currents on the wire. I had a habit of doing so, you know, of listening—In the quiet. Little by little the silence would become—complicated. One might say. I passed whole nights just sitting up and listening like this. And I heard things Bell. Signals. There was one I heard again and again. A snap, followed by a grating sound that lasted two or three seconds. And then it faded into silence. And. There was another one like the chirping of a bird. This was before the trolley car, Bell. Before electric light. This was when the only electric circuits in constant use were the telegraph wires. And they went quiet at night. Bell. So I was able to hear these. Delicate things.

B Watson.

W I could hear the strays. I could hear other currents. Other transmissions. That repeated. That were quite distinct. At the time I thought perhaps. That the currents causing these sounds came from—well, from explosions on the sun. Or. That they were—signals. From another planet.

B Why did you never tell me.

W I didn't have time. Because of electricity. Very quickly Bell, the more delicate sounds were completely drowned out. By all the electric light and power dynamos. And I didn't want to tell you too soon because. You might have laughed.

B I certainly would not have laughed.

W   You might have.

B   Perhaps. Perhaps not.

W   But I never found out—

B   You have a sensitive ear.

W   I could tell the difference between one current
          and another Bell. Even one current of static from
          another. I could discern what is in it Bell. What
          MORE was in it. As though it were. A. Golden
          thread.

B   You might have heard—winds, or. Or weather.

W   I heard winds and weather, yes. But Bell, there
          was more than that. It was.. What if. What if it
          was another planet. Or this one. A resonance of.
          Of. Life itself.

B   Well what would that mean then.

W   Well?

B   Watson—

W   Knowing what the world is.

B   And then what—

BLACKOUT

~~~~~~~~~~~~~~~~~~~~

I AM THE LILAC NEW-RED SEA WONDER AND THE BLUE

I AM THE LILAC NEW-RED SEA WONDER AND THE BLUE

IRREPLACEABLE

I AM SOCRATES

I AM A SOCRATES

THEREFORE THE STATE WILL TERMINATE ME

THE END WILL COME OUT OF MY MOUTH

THE END

CAME INTO ME AND THEREFORE

OUT OF ME

YES

LAMP? I LIGHT THE LAMP. I AM IT.

I LIGHT IT BY ELECTRICITY

YES

I LIGHT THE LAMP ALSO BY KEROSENE

I KNOW THE POWER WORDS

I KNOW THEIR MEANINGS

BECAUSE

MEANINGS ARE UNIVERSAL

POSSESSING A PORTION OF THE UNIVERSAL

IS AS GOOD AS POSSESSING ALL

BECAUSE

SPEECH IS SILVER

SILENCE IS GOLDEN

NOW

I AM STILL SOCRATES

IRREPLACEABLE AND THEREFORE CHINESE

WHICH IS TO SAY

IT IS WONDERFUL TO BE ADMIRED

IT IS WONDERFUL TO BE ON TOP

WHEN ONE IS IN BETWEEN

EVEN WHEN I AM DOWN BELOW I CAN SEE FOR MILES

BEING BABETTE I AM A SWITZERLAND

I AM WELL-KNOWN AS AN EGYPTIAN

MOREOVER EVERYDAY CABINET MINISTERS CALL TO
ME IN THE STREET

THEY KNOW MY WORK

THEY ARE MY STUDENTS

SOON THEY WILL GRANT ME THE MONOPOLY

THEY KNOW IT IS OWED ME

YOU KNOW

I AM AN ALP

I AM TALL AND WHITE

WHEN ONE HAS BEEN GREAT AND THEN BECOMES
LITTLE IT IS A LOSS

LOSS SIGNIFIES

PEOPLE LOVE ONLY THEMSELVES

ONLY THEMSELVES

BEING BABETTE I KNOW

THAT TO LOVE ANOTHER IS A CALCULUS

BUT BEING BABETTE I ALSO KNOW

THAT OTHERS ARE NOT ME

THEY MUST BE FAR BELOW

NEVERTHELESS

THESE PEOPLE WILL HELP ME COLLECT MY REWARD

I AM ROYALLY LOVELY, SO LOVELY AND SO PURE

TWO MAGNATES BEG ME TO MARRY THEM DAILY

EACH ONE OFF TO ONE SIDE

LARGE THEY ARE NOT

THEY ARE MENTAL GIANTS

ADDITIONALLY

I KNOW WHAT IT MEANS TO BE ADMIRED

FAILURES LOVE TO ADMIRE ME

BUT FAILED PEOPLE DO NOT BELONG TO ME

ADMIRATION IS LIKE CALUMNY

AND CALUMNY IS LIKE JEALOUSY

ONCE I WAS SLANDERED BY SOMEBODY BECAUSE I
ALWAYS CARRIED CATS IN MY ARMS

I CANNOT BE BLAMED IF I AM ADORED

LISTEN TO ME

LISTEN TO ME

I KNOW PERFECTLY WELL

WE ARE THE STOVES FOR THE STATE

BUT I AM THE INHERITOR

AND THE INHERITRIX

OF INTEREST-DRAUGHTS

IT IS A JUST SYSTEM

I ESTABLISH UPHOLSTERED FURNITURE

I POSITION IT ABSOLUTELY

EACH NIGHT I AM TORMENTED

BY ODORS AND CALLS

BUT I BEAR IT

EVERY NIGHT SOMEBODY IN THE NEIGHBORING
QUARTER

SHOOTS HIS ODOR THROUGH MY WINDOW

THAT QUARTER AND ALL QUARTERS EXIST FOR A
REASON

THEY RESEMBLE shit AND THEREFORE DO NOT
DESERVE WHAT THEY DO NOT HAVE

IT IS A JUST SYSTEM

THEY DO NOT KNOW IT

THEY SLANDER ME

BECAUSE BEING BABETTE I UNDERSTAND

IT IS PERFECTLY SIMPLE IT IS UNDERSTANDABLE

BECAUSE I AM A DOUBLE POLYTECHNIC

IRREPLACEABLE

I SUFFER HIEROGLYPHICAL. Look. Marie said I should
stay in the other ward today, Ida said she couldn't even do
the mending—it was only kind of me to do the mending—I
am the only Babette in this house and my work is never
done—look—I am in my house and the others live with
me—on MY charity—I AFFIRM THE ASYLUM SIXFOLD
and I bless it because the end of it came out of my mouth
not that it is my caprice to remain here.

They forced me to remain here—I have also affirmed a
house of four storeys, sixteen windows across and four
up to the cornices—It is there I entertain my company in
silence—WE NEED WHAT WE UNDERSTAND

naturally

THIS EQUALS JUSTICE

What. What. What. You don't understand what. What.
What. Listen. I was shut up—

No. No. I was shut up for FOURTEEN YEARS. That means
SHUT UP for fourteen years SO THAT MY BREATH COULD
NOT COME OUT ANYWHERE LET ME FINISH

I am explaining it to you. That is hieroglyphical suffering—
that is the very HIGHEST suffering—that not even the
breath could come out—they did this to me repeatedly
for FOURTEEN YEARS but THEY KNOW. I was the one
they wanted because I ESTABLISH EVERYTHING and
they know I don't even belong in such a little room—
that is hieroglyphical suffering—in a black dark black
box you have to see me and then you immediately

understand, I have demanded my freedom for I am known internationally—the highest beauty and the greatest works—I have told the world when my breath could not come out—they shut me up and pretended to forget me but I reminded them I told them through the speaking-tubes that went from inside to outside—

I told them and they know now

They know for good

I AM SOCRATES

Recording: No. no. no. no. Um no. Ah no. NO. no {etc}

IT IS WIDELY KNOWN
I AM A MISS
BUT I AM A HIT
I AM MISS SAINT

I ESTABLISH THE CLARITY THEREFORE ALL THIS
GOES WITH ME

Pupil—books—wisdom—modesty—no words to express this wisdom—not approximate—THIS is the highest ground-pedestal—his teachings had to die because of wicked men—AND SO IT WAS TO BE FOR ME—immortality—falsely accused—to be falsely accused is the highest—sublimest sublimity—self-satisfied—that is all Socrates—the fine learned world—I ATTAINED IT I never cut a thread—I was the best dressmaker NEVER CUT A THREAD never dropped a bit of cloth on the floor—fine nimble fingers —fine world of art—ART is a bluff—they pushed me in my chair up onto the bluff—salt winds—it was the bluff of art—I knew—they had made facsimiles—their spyings—they thought I had erected it in my mind—but I am more refined than they are—THERE EXISTS A

FINE PROFESSORSHIP—I hold it—THEREFORE I hold
it—the university holds open my chair—I cannot occupy
it—I occupy it but I am PREVENTED—THEREFORE.
NEVERTHELESS. THEREFORE I excel at a petticoat—
twenty-five francs—never another like it—that is the
highest—in prison they deserve what they get but I—
slandered by wicked men—halfwits—longshoremen—
garbage—I am explaining it to you but you have to let me
because

THIS IS PARALYSIS. THAT WAS. What is. That is BAD
FOOD—overwork—sleep deprivation—machinery—natural
causes—consumption—once i coughed and out came a
baby and kittens—now they orchestrate my spine—the
paralysis comes from there—wheel-chair—console—
EVERYBODY KNOWS wheel-chairs are not the only
paralysis nor are they the worst—my situation expresses
itself in UNIQUE pains—IRREPLACEABLE PAINS—that
is the way it has always been with me—woe is never
far away—I suffer the highest woes in the world and I
THEREFORE belong to the monopoly, to the payment—the
payment belongs to me—

—but ONLY liquid— paper—love—paper is like money—
money is therefore an organ—the highest bank notes—
shrill to the height of my head—it is HERE that the
suffering is affirmed—inside my—telephone—*rubs a part
of her body*—I agreed to suffer for them it is my generosity
it is why the people love me it is why it is THEREFORE
a just system FOREVER—I agreed to suffer as universal
mother—I agreed to crutches and they followed me
with their eyes—I AGREED TO CRUTCHES AND THEY
FOLLOWED ME WITH THEIR EYES THEY HEARD ME
DRAG MY BODY ACROSS THE FLOOR
JUST LISTEN
I NEED IMMEDIATE HELP

Recording: No. no. no. no. Um no. Ah no. NO. no {etc}

She looks up, she looks for where the voice is coming from. It deflates and withers her. She stares vacuously.

No you. No you. No YOU. It's YOU. YOU. YOU. I am the only responsible party. I am the only one. I AM RESPONSIBLE TO CARE FOR THEM. IT IS MY GENEROSITY AND MY SWEET REWARD. Discords—it is really a crime—and now I have to be cared for—I must be cared for—this is a DISCORD that preceded me this is a DISCORD that by my power I affirmed and buried. It is simple. I saw two people twisting cords in the loft— everybody knows that in the world there are only two such great discords AND I SAW THEM—they live above me and it is they who installed the speaking-tubes but they knew I had no breath—I am the picture of health because I have to be cared for—When they come to care for me I show my world owner face AND MY WORLD OWNER-ESS FACE—I ESTABLISH DISCORDS simply WON'T GO any longer on this floor—No not on this floor—A dowager empress could eat off this floor—it is under my care—being Babette I know how to care—being Babette my body is like a chair for children—they should have followed my example-- there is such a great discord that they don't want to care for me—in any case they cannot—they were making lace in the loft and only went on working without once thinking of me—They twisted a bundle of cords and wires, but I WAS NOT BORN YESTERDAY AND I KNOW all discords come from negligence—Now I am attached to them—Everybody knows discords DO NOT belong to this floor. Discords are for Siberia—nothing could be more obvious—it is high time I was cared for—I have consumption from this regime—I never know when it will come out—you never know what will come out—LISTEN TO ME—*clenched teeth*—instead of providing me with the deed and title they only go on

working—BUT THEY ARE NOT WORKING both making
lace in the loft but everybody knows it was a bundle of
wires and cords but I knew for years what they were doing
and all those people who followed my progress—MY
PROGRESS HAS BEEN PUBLISHED IN PROSE AND
VERSE MY PROGRESS HAS BEEN PUBLISHED AND
ADMIRED and everybody knows

I COME FIRST
WITH THE DEAF AND DUMB MISTER W
FROM THE CITY AND THEN THE COUNTRY
Mister W from the city comes to me here and marries
me here—to guard against perversities I shall tell you—a
Mister Grimm—he thought he was Mister W but he
wasn't—When he came I as Babette established the
churches in the city to guard the money—THE MONEY IS
ALWAYS IN THE ORGAN—This was already 20 years ago—
in particular the organ at St. Peter's the most famous one
belongs to me—Mister K the nephew of M who everybody
knows is a close associate of, of, of, of, of, of, Mister K
in M the nephew of M HOOO manages my mo HOOOO
manages my money in Saint Peter'sHOOO, then wouldn't
you knowHOOO.

I see the deaf and dumb Mister W walking across the
square near Saint Peter's on a Sunday—Mister W can give
information to anyone who asks Mister WHOOO always
accounts to the very last penny that belongs to me—Mister
W belongs to the city and to no master—I belong to the
monopoly the notary HOOO knows I come first with the
deaf and dumb Mister W from the city and NO MASTER—
THAT IS DOUBLE—IT IS OBVIOUS THAT IS DOUBLE AND
SAME WEIGHT HOOO—

BUT NO SOONER HAD I AFFIRMED MY ONE THOUSAND
MILLIONS that—*blushing, bashful*—uh uh oh oh you
cannot believe—the littlest the greenest warmest little

green snake—it was so little and warm and looking down I
saw it come up to my mouth—IT BELONGED TO GRIMM
and SIMULTANEOUSLY to the Czar and Kaiser—I could
see it had human reason and its open mouth produced a
tongue— it wanted to tell me something—It was so close
I had no choice but to perspire—everyone who saw it has
written that it wanted to kiss me and this is extremely well-
known

*Silence. Miss St is now an extension of the silence. She
looks up and listens. Like a dog or squirrel observing a
change in the weather. She loses confidence again. Stares
vacuously, looks down and picks a scab.*

Softly, sadly to herself

Speech is silver
Silence is golden

Everybody knows silver stars—liquid flows—silver flows—
this is why money is made from silver—supply of money—
THE LIQUID SUPPLY IS THE HIGHEST—I sold the largest
silver island in the world and it was returned to me—silver
medals—ONE MUST CLING TO WHAT ONE MAKES—that
is love—to cling requires watches—silver boxes—goblets—
spoons—coats—petticoats—but for that I had no choice
but to restructure the face—the maid had imagined it
poorly—No matter what I crowned highest eloquence—all
who were there heard me—all who were there knew it
was FINALITY—as owner of the world the mightiest silver
island in the world belongs to me—but I afterwards gave
the order to supply ONLY MONEY NO OBJECTS—silver is
smooth—flows—love—all the existing silverware must be
melted down into money--

NOT YOU. NOT. NOW YOU. Now YOU

YOU ARE TOO UGLY TO BE TRUE

—so the rest of us must stay high on the hill—His face
emptied out for public safety—had to be so—This is the
most UP I have been—I AM THE MOST UP THAT CAN
HAVE BEEN—I am pierced above and below because
my radiance passes through me—Upscale—SEE IT
PASSING—Most high—feeling is reserved for the highest—
is the highest class—my class—HEAVENLY RADIANCE
TRANSPIRING—aeronautics ALSO belonging only to me—
It is a fact often discussed by THE HIGHEST SOCIETY
though the common people know nothing about it—
Nothing could be more obvious—those who care to know
are those are worth knowing are those who know

I AM TRIPLE OWNER OF THE WORLD

THEREFORE DO I AFFIRM SINGLY DOUBLY TRIPLY

Grand hotel-- hotel life—omnibuses—theatres—comedies–
parks–carriages–fiacres–trams—traffic –houses—stations—
steamships—seamstresses—railways—cinema—post—
telegraph—national holidays—music—stores—libraries—
governments—letters—monograms—muscles—postcards—
gondolas—delegates—dinners—payments—gentry—
coaches—Negro on the box—flags—nations—one horse
carriage—pavilion—education——gold—diplomacy—
fuel—pearls—rings—diamonds—coal—central court—
credit office—villa—servants and maids—carpets—
curtains—mirrors—

BUT
BUT IT IS OBVIOUS. IT IS VISIBLE IN THIS
GRACIOUSNESS.
YOU HAVE ONLY TO LOOK TO SEE AND YOU CAN HEAR
ME.
I AM THE BELL THE NOTE-FACTORY THE MONOPOLY

PROGRESS EXPRESSES ITSELF IN ME
PROGRESS BECOMES FINALITY
BEING BABETTE I AM SOCRATES
I AM WHAT IS SAID
IN THE WORLD ARE THINGS
THAT ARE NOT ME
I SUFFER
I AM ON TOP OF THE WORLD
BUT THE WORLD IS ROUND

—I saw it a thousandfold—that is paralysis—
PREEMINENCE— I saw a note-factory seven storeys
high—it was double I TOLD YOU a front one WINDOWS
CORNICE THE WIRES GO THROUGH THERE and behind
it is the water closet—like a man the note-factory is always
double—there I straddled the lower part—what a relief I
told the queen what a relief—

NOW LISTEN.

I DO NOT DO.
I AM.

HERE BY NECESSITY I INCLUDE EVERYTHING THAT
CAN HAPPEN

IT IS MY WORLD—I CANNOT FORSAKE IT—you would
feel as i do were you in my position—BUT YOU CANNOT
BE IN MY POSITION—they are preparing to afflict me—
AMASSING—continually improving all diseases which
are caused by chemical productions, poisonings so that
I can never see anyone—then they launch attacks of
suffocation—from above as has been credibly reported
more than once—they begin from above and then they
make an account of what is lodged in me—each time it
is the same--then the terrible stretchings—they stretch
me every single time—they stretch me—all the cracked

parts are left thereafter to themselves—I am responsible
to assimilate them—BELIEVE ME on this food you cannot
get a figure like mine—look at me and consider—I find
another way to insert my food—I have no choice because
of their preexisting awful system—EVERY LIVING PERSON
HAS FELT THIS AT LEAST ONCE— when there were tons
of iron plate lying on your back—then the poisoning—is
interior—is shot in through the window—then, as if you
were in ice—they organize pains in your back—this belongs
to my suffering for which I am inevitably paid with liquid
currency—wet silver in the sunshine—ENCLOSED ME—
THE MISTER MASTER—BYE BYE BABETTE—EAT THIS
BABETTE—BE THIS BE THAT BABETTE—BECAUSE—
because of the monopoly—everyone knows the monopoly—
so they can keep me attached they established a system to
falsify my previously-established system because I am the
precedent of the system and the monopoly which BY THE
WAY is not the highest monopoly the operator promised to
pay me eighty thousand francs nine years ago in exchange
for listening to every single thing I said—

I am wealthy because I had to endure such pains—all
suffering has a silver lining—all branches of government
know my details—common knowledge—I am known to
need immediate help and it is promised to me—those in
power know me and their friends know me—they call out to
me—they want to greet me—they thank me—the delay will
not kill me because monopoly is a finality of all innovations
since 1886, chemical productions, ventilations, sleep-
deprivation—I innovated the monopoly that listens in on
me—even without that a government would be obliged
to stand by me with immediate help—I did establish a
note-factory—this cannot be denied—even if I weren't
owner of the world the government would still have to bring
help—as owner of the world I should have already danced
six quadrilles each with the several gentlemen who have
been asking for me daily since 1866—they came each day

to the lobby and waited for me but I was prevented I was
SINGLED THEY SHUT ME IN the room with the shit smell
because they knew GENTLEMEN MAKE THEMSELVES
MINE SINCE 1886 they shut me up because they want
what's mine—because you have reason you can understand

All those who endure such sufferings should be helped,
this is the universal principle, all those who endure are to
be welcomed into the MONOPOLY—

this is how it is

AS UNIVERSAL BABETTE I AM WELL KNOWN
I am known in the SLICKER QUARTERS to have the
highest constitution belonging to a man—in spite of
this I am female—No powder belongs to me—I do not
require—Creams—A salve—Upward motion only rubbing in
this articulation is permitted-- I originate my own powder
or I find it in the floor—It is how I keep my figure—And
moreover mine is the kind of blood too beautiful for powder
in my belly there is no room and under my sash I refuse it I
keep my cheeks pink in order to always be ready—

BECAUSE I AM THE ONLY IRREPLACEABLE—

Recording: NO. NO. UH. NO. NO. {etc}

I am. I am.
I AM DOUBLE POLYTECHNIC
YOU LIE
YOU ARE A LIAR TO DENY IT
I am THE—
THE highest, all-highest—I am that—I am it-- the
highest I of dressmaking—YOU KNOW IT—the highest
achievement—the highest intelligence AS WAS PROVED
IN THE EXAMINATION I PASSED IT HIGHER THAN HAS
EVER BEEN RECORDED—the highest achievement in the

culinary art—YOU—you—HAD A BABY—PACKAGED IT—
PUT IT IN SHIT—the highest achievement in all spheres—
the double polytechnic is irreplaceable—the universal with
twenty thousand francs—never cut a thread—fine world of
art—CLIT ROT CUT BUTT—not apply a thread of trimming
where it is not seen—plum tart with corn-meal crust—
FAT HANDS SADDLE BAG HAG—it is of the greatest
importance—finest professorship—TOUGH TITTIE HAG
is a doubloon—twenty-five francs—Schneckenmuseum
clothing is the highest— salon and bedroom—should live
there as double polytechnic because I am the

Recording: NO NO NO NO NO NO NO NO

BUT NATURAL END I AM YES I AM THE MASTER KEY
because the master-key is the house key—I am not the
house-key but the house—I am most often the master—I
AM ALSO MISTER MASTER the house belongs to me—
yes I am the master-key—I affirm the master-key as my
property—it is therefore a house-key that folds up—a
key that unlocks all doors—therefore it includes the
house—it is a keystone—monopoly—BECAUSE I AM THE
UNIVERSAL—

This is what I am trying to explain to you. NOW IT IS
YOUR TURN TO BE PATIENT. Listen. There now. You
see, it is like this.

I came as the universal seventeen years ago—naturally
under regular conditions—everything must be taken into
account when the universal becomes you—you must
tabulate all inheritances titles and deeds, totality of
financial circumstances too—title of world owner includes
one thousand millions—that is the villa, here is my
equipage—I've been riding horseback and driving since
1866—You see I know how to hold the crop because I
worship liberty—After all I've been universal since the

death of my father—in the winter months too I affirm the
universal—even if I'd not affirmed it before the crowds they
would have known it—my heart is open on account of my
inheritance and the unofficial machines that have been
installed—twenty five thousand at the very least—with
what emphasis—the Swiss annuity is one hundred and fifty
thousand—the heathens chatter so—they said that Mister
O had drawn my annuity—gossip—universal is a finality—
you can be that through deceased persons—through
legacies—universal is property—the property belongs to
me—
Because you see—

I AM A FAMOUS JEWESS SINCE 1866

Since then it has all come to me—
I belong to the synagogue in Lowenstrasase since 1866
AND I am a Jewess since 1866 AND YOU KNOW IT YOU
KNOW IT—Babette is a famous Jewish name—moreover
YOU KNOW IT—as owner of the world I am therefore three
empresses—I am also Maria Theresa as von Planta—that is
finality—

I AM HERO OF THE PEN
TAKE THIS DOWN
ONCE AND FOR ALL
THIS IS THE NATURAL WORLD
THIS IS THE SIMPLICITY OF FINALITY

Generosity—forbearance—heroic deed—the content of
what one writes—the highest intelligence—the highest
traits of character—highest endurance—highest noblesse—
the highest that the world shows—includes in itself—
letters—deeds of purchase and transfer—FINALITY—
Alliance, counter-bill, conclusions, signature, title deed,
procuration—

Generally includes the key too—foreign currency—
dedication—worship—I AM AWARE that the worship,
veneration, and admiration of which I am worthy cannot
be offered to me—so wanders the noblest of women,
with roses she would like to surround the people—Queen
Louise of Prussia—I established that long ago—POOP IN
PIT I am her—those are the highest conclusions in life—
KEYSTONE—*stares vaculously*

a shift in the air
distortion

AND STILL AFTER ALL THIS TIME
YOU DO NOT KNOW ME
YOU MISTAKE THE OTHER ONE FOR ME
HEAR ME NOW
KNOW NOW
AND KNOW THE ONE FINALITY
THIS IS THE FINAL THING
THAT
I AM THE FINEST TURKEY
IF YOU PLEASE

It is simple to see how obviously I belong to the FINEST
Turkey IN THE WORLD—NO OTHER WOMAN IN THE
WORLD SHOULD BE UNDRESSED—I am capable of being
undressed for I know the thrill of the artist—this figure
and I own international renown—THE NATURAL IS THE
HIGHEST HEALTH pearls and corsetry the sunny airs—I
am the ADMINISTRATOR of cold champagne and the
strongest black wine—all of the finest produce—we are the
mightiest preservers of the world—Switzerland comes to
my side as the mightiest most glorious nation—Switzerland
expresses herself in Turkey—INSERTED Turkey swells,
Turkey swells and expresses the most enormous worlds—
morphines stop up the holes occasioned—BECAUSE
Turkey is fine and imports the finest foodstuffs—fine

wines—cigars—lots of coffee—dates—figs—pearls—
creams—rosewater—yellow oil—sesame—bells, tiny
bells—preserved animals PRESERVED FOR MY BEAUTY—
double bazaar—

NATURALLY NATURE IS DESIGNED TO BE EXTRACTED

double bazaar I FAMOUSLY affirm two bazaars—one bazaar
above and one bazaar below—ladies' handiwork—the
most wonderful plate, glassware, all jewelry, toilet soaps,
purses——BECAUSE they are Czars, the sons of the
highest in Russia, dressed up as Czars—the bazaars are
extraordinarily good businesses—Czars are hired for these
businesses, the Russians have the most virile businesses,
they have their incomes from these bazaars because they
are sons of world-owners and world-owneresses—once I
coughted and a little girl jumped out of my mouth with
a little brown frock and a little black apron—my little
daughter—the deputy—shot out of my mouth to the end
of the lunatic asylum—she was slightly paralyzed—sewn
together from rags—she belongs to a bazaar—you know,
these businesses have a high turnover—ultimately ends
in wealth—I came first as double, as sole owner of the
world, first with the deaf and dumb Mister W from the
city and NO MASTER—I AM THE FINAL MASTER and
then—and then—and meanwhile –THE double bazaar—
and meanwhile—I never hesitate—He tried to court
me—I am not cavalier but kind—I know who is listening
AND WHO HEARS—If I did not know then how would I
have survived SO LONG UNDER THIS REGIME—I AM A
PALESTINE—but by my power I ACHIEVED COMPLETION
OF PLANETARY HEALTH—

I KNEW what to do NOT TO BE KILLED

DIDN'T I

DIDN'T I

I KNEW AND I REQUIRED

A MILLION AND A DOCTOR

ANNUITY AND DEPUTY

I WAS FAMOUS ENOUGH TO HAVE IT ALL

AND THE BLUFF TOO

MORE THAN ENOUGH TO ESTABLISH WHAT IS TRUE IN
LIFE

EVEN YOU CANNOT DENY YOU HAVE AT LEAST TWO
SIDES

You can take your health into your own hands
Will-power makes such a difference
FINALITY OF HUMAN HEALTH VIBRATES IN ME
The doctor said it to me once in a crowd and once behind
the stair
I AM SUCH A WOMAN
I AM SO MADE
RICHEST CONFIDENCES AND KISSES ON THE THROAT
HE IN ME ARE THE FINAL THREE AND I NOW DWELL IN
THE TOTALITY
THE ORIGINAL IS COMPLETENESS
ACHIEVED BY ME
BUT
BECAUSE
BUT
BECAUSE
I CREATED THE HIGHEST MOUNTAIN PEAK AND
I HAVE ACHIEVED THE HIGHEST OF ALL MOUNTAIN
PEAKS

BY MENDING—HIGHER THAN A SUGAR CONE ON THE
TONGUE
THE PUBLIC KNOWS
ONCE YOU HAVE ACHIEVED THIS IT IS OUT OF THE
QUESTION THAT YOU SHOULD BE KILLED—

Sound

Blackout

Sound

03   Lovers

~~~~~~~~~~~~~

A OK—he's listening.

B **recording:** *a toddler half-singing half-telling a story. for example:*

Once upon a time there were two bunny rabbits. They were friends. One day they went... to see the elephants jump over a fence. But the watery grave wasn't so tall. So they slipped. And fell. And the little one laughed and... the little tickie went wickety wickety. The end!

b

A   Hang on a second

        silence

A   Okay. I'm back.

c

*fragments of phone conversations
all, variously:*

"Uh-huh,"

"Right

," "Yeah

," "Okay

," etc.

A   How did it go today.

B   Great.

A   Great.

B   Yeah.

A   *silence*

B   She's really the whole package.

A   Really. The whole package?

B   Yeah. She's the whole package.

A   Great.

         silence
         silence
         silence

A   So—

A   Say something?

B   What do you want me to say.

A   Anything. Say what you want to say.

silence

B   I think there's a difference between World and Planet.

A   Yeah. Probably.

B   But I basically think it's too late.

A   What about culture.

B   What about it.

A   Will culture save the world.

B   Definitely not.

A   Really?

B   I don't know. I mean. Culture is the world.

A   Uhm

A   Everything's good with us, yeah.

silence

Oh I don't know.

silence

I guess her quirks. Her personal habits. Are starting to lose their charisma somewhat. But—

A   What are you doing.

B   Nothing

silence
silence
silence

A   Um

silence

A   Well. What did you mean. Last night. When you
said you felt weird.

silence

B   I just felt. Beholden to you.

A   Is that why you didn't wanna talk.

B   Yeah. I just felt weird. And I didn't want to feel.
Beholden to you.

A   Oh.

B   *silence*

A   What do you mean by beholden.

silence
silence
silence

B   I don't know.

A   I don't want to talk about the past anymore

B   What else is there to talk about.

A   What are you wearing.

        uncomfortable laughter

B   I don't know. Nothing. Pants and a shirt.

A   I wish I could see you.

B   What are you wearing.

A   I look like shit.

j

A   I want to die.

B   Seriously.

A   The world is so fucked.

B   I know.

A   I know.

B   What's the weather like.

A   Disgusting.

silence silence silence

B   Oh.

silence silence silence

A   I'm doing what I have to do.

B   I know you are baby.

silence silence silence

B   What did you do last night.

A   Last night. *silence* Oh I jacked off & went to sleep.

B   *tight* Cute.

A   There's this one actor who looks like you. I'm kind of addicted.

B   Oh uh cute
A   The rest of them all look the same.

B   No they don't. But. Well I guess so kind of.

A   I'm surprised it still works.

B   It's kind of eternal.

A   Yeah.

B   Listen, I have to get up really early tomorrow—

I

B   But I'm into that. You know. I'm into you in
control. You taking charge. I like it. It, ah,
it relaxes me. You know.. I don't have to do
anything. I don't have to guess anything. It's not
like you're actually a rapist. Or anything like that.
I just like the. You know. The drama.

A   Uh

A   What's the matter with you.

B   I don't know. Like.

n

A   Okay. Let's all take a deep breath. Inhale. Exhale.
Excellent. One more time all together. *inhale.*
exhale. That was great.

O

A   Good. Now put the hood on.

B   Again?

A   Put it on

silence
silence

Is it on?

B   mmmffff

A   Sit so I can see you.

silence

Good. Now say my name.

B   mmffffmmmffffmmmmffff

A   Excellent. *silence* Now repeat after me.

I fucking hate myself.

B   ffsdfsdsdfsdfsdfsdfsdfsdfsf

A   My cock is a skinny turd and I am the worst and final shit of my mother

B   mgcdtmhvmfgdfertmfgdtrksfdgjdtertsiuhfgjksgh sdfjgherugisur

A   I'm yours.

B   sdfsnjfsdfkw

A   I'm yours. I'm nothing without you.

p

A Do you remember the first time I wrote you

B Yeah

A What did I write you

B You sent me a poem

A Right right

B ""lip pelts. cake and ale. salsa. sours. cigarettes."

silence silence silence

i knew i had to know you

A yeah well I used to be beautiful

B You're still beautiful.

A uh

B You're beautiful. I can hear it.

A I'm lost

B Write to me.

A Can't I just talk to you.

B Of course of course. Sorry. Of course. I just meant—I miss you. *silence silence silence* I'm listening.

silence
silence
silence

A   Uhm—

silence
silence
silence

A   I don't want to explain myself.

B   Okay

A   I just

silence
silence
silence

I just. I just want to talk to somebody who already understands me. I want to talk to somebody who feels me.

B   Do you have an idea of who this person might be?

A   Well? You maybe? *silence silence silence* Uhm.

taut. A is tight tight tight with hate and fear and
love. B is tight tight tight with rage and fear.

A   Dad?

B   Hello.

A   Hi Dad.

B   Hi.

A   What's up.

B   *silence silence silence* We just finished dinner.
The girls are watching a movie.

A   That's nice.

silence
silence
silence

A   Dad

B   Yes

A   Is it nice to hear my voice

silence
silence
silence
silence
silence
silence

B   yes

S

A   But if you. If you wanted me then

B   I do want you. Come on.

A   But if you really did then.

B   Then what.

A   I don't know. You would come over. You would
        call. I'm always the one to call.

B   Oh come on. I call you.

A   You don't. I pay attention. You don't.

B   Well what do you want me to say.

A   I miss you I love you so much I can't stand being
        apart from you I'm coming over right now.

B   Well. I do. All of those things.

A   But I said it. I'm the one who said it.

B   So? That doesn't make it not true.

A   Uh.

t

A	You say goodbye first
B	No you
A	No. I said it first
B	Ok
	silence *silence* *silence*
B	Hello?
A	Hi!
B	Hi!
A	Ok
B	Ok
A+B	One, two three—

A   I call his number.

B   It still works?

A   It goes to voicemail. I sing to him.

B   O god.

A   I write to him. I live in civilization. I want something amazing to happen. Everything is transparent. Everything is visible. Nothing is cured. I want to be held responsible. I want to be empty. I write to him because I'm so fucked and it's my fault. I call him I feel like a terrorist. Because I don't even exist. Where is he. Where is he.

B   Sweetheart. Sweetheart.

A   I can't even say his name anymore I'm so fucked. And saying it is lying. But I have to say something. I just wish I could sleep. I wish I could sleep. I just wish I could sleep.

A   Look you're supposed to be listening to me not
interrogating me.

B   *You* were interrogating *me*.

A   Sorry.

silence
silence
silence

*An extremely loud, violent, obscene argument
between a woman and two men is happening
offstage and continues throughout the scene. As
though coming from the street five or six storeys
below the bedroom of an apartment. Screaming.
Threats. Breaking glass. Is this a physical fight or
not. It sounds severe. It's fascinating.*

A+B *open eyes. groggy. blink some. listening. they
want to go back to sleep. thick with sleep. stare
vacuously. intense listening, trying to make out
what they hear. extreme physical tension thick
with sleep.*

A When did I fall asleep

B Hard to say

A When did you fall asleep

C A little after you

*plenty of heavy space, time between lines.
pregnant silence. A+B listening. disgust, anxiety.
fascination, stupor. part of what they feel is: does
this have to mean something about us or not.*

C Did we fuck again

A+B No

A   Do you want to listen to some music.

B   That would mean lying to ourselves

C   We could call the cops

B   The cops are assholes

A   We could pour water on them

B   I don't think that would help them

B   If people can't scream in the street then where can they scream

A   I want them to shut up

A   We should record them

C   I love the sound of people's voices

A   *silence silence silence*

I don't know.

silence

I just wanted something exciting to happen. I would have done hair removal.

silence

I hate my job.

A   I haven't heard from her in weeks.

B   Where is she.

A   I guess she's still around.

B   Does she have any money.

A   She must. If she didn't she'd call.

Z

A   My dear little girl

You must not scold me this once if I do sit up for a moment even though it is late—to write a few lines to you.

I little thought when I went to Cambridge this afternoon—of the surprise in store for me. You seemed to me to be drifting away from me – so far away—with Visible Speech and ever so many things between – and I almost despaired of ever reaching you.

I little thought how near you were. I can scarcely believe now that you really and truly love me – and that you will be my wife. I am afraid to go to sleep lest I should find it all a dream – so I shall lie awake and think of you.

It is so cold and selfish living all for oneself. A man is only half a man who has no one to love and to cherish. "A delicate hot house plant" (like you – is far more valuable to me than one that can stand the storms and buffets of this rude world alone. It will be my pride and delight —Mabe—to protect and to love you. Don't go from me any more.

May God guide us both so that we may be a comfort and support to each other.

Yours and yours only—

A	Hi little one.
B	Oh my god.
A	Hi darling
B	Oh my god. Oh my god.
A	It's me.
B	Oh my god. Oh my god.
A	It's me.
B	I know. I know. I know it's you.
A	Hi darling.
B	Where are you.
A	I'm here.
B	Oh my god. Where are you.
A	I'm here baby. I'm right here.

Everything

Goes

Black

ACKNOWLEDGMENTS

‿‿‿‿‿‿‿‿‿‿‿‿‿‿

TELEPHONE, inspired by *The Telephone Book* by Avital Ronell, was commissioned by The Foundry Theatre in 2008 and first produced at The Cherry Lane Theatre in February 2009.

The director was Ken Rus Schmoll, with Matthew Dellapina as Watson, Gibson Frazier as Bell, and Birgit Huppuch as Miss St. Set design by Marsha Ginsberg. Lighting design by Tyler Micoleau. Sound design by Matt Hubbs. Costume design by Carol Bailey. The stage manager was Molly Eustis.

WATSON+BELL is based, in part, on *Exploring Life: The Autopbiography of Thomas A. Watson* by Thomas A. Watson (1926) and on The Alexander Graham Bell Family Papers at the Library of Congress, available online.

MISS ST'S HIEROGLYPHIC SUFFERING is based, in part, on *The Psychology of Dementia Praecox* by Carl Jung.

LOVERS includes, in scene p, quotations from a poem by Jason Burns and, in scene z, a letter from Alexander Graham Bell to his then-fiancée Mabel Hubbard.

Special thanks to Melanie Joseph, Sunder Ganglani, Amy Kaissar, the ENVISIONretreat at Bard, and Chris Kraus.